A catalogue record for this book is available from the British Library
Published by Ladybird Books Ltd
80 Strand London WC2R ORL
A Penguin Company

1 3 5 7 9 10 8 6 4 2

© LADYBIRD BOOKS LTD MMIV

Huge Henry

written by Mandy Ross
illustrated by John Haslam

Huge Henry wasn't very happy. Try as he might, he could not make trumpety sounds. All he could do was flap his ears all day.

"It's not fair," he grumbled. "I want to make loud jungle music."

Off he stomped to the watering hole.

Down by the river, Henry heard
Muddy Molly gurgling in the water.
Gloopety-bloop, gloopety-bloop!

"That's jungle music!" he boomed.
And then he had an idea...

"It doesn't matter if I can't trumpet. I'm going to start a jungle band!"

"Great idea!" gurgled Molly.

"I'll call when it's time to start," said Henry, and he set off into the trees.

He hadn't gone far when he heard a tiny TWEETY TWEET!

Henry's huge ears flapped.

"Wait! Wait!" chirruped Birdy.
"TWEETY TWEET! Can I join the
jungle band?"

"Of course!" boomed Henry in his
huge voice.
"I'll call you when it's time to start."
And he set off again.

A little further on, Henry heard a
squiggly hiss in the undergrowth.

His huge ears flapped.
"More jungle music!"

"It's me," said Hissing Hattie. "I've heard about your band. Please can I join?"

"Of course!" boomed Henry.
"I'll call you when it's time to start."
And he went on his way.

He hadn't gone much further when he heard a ROARING and a BOOMING.

Henry's huge ears flapped.
"More jungle music?"

"Good morning!" roared
Roaring Rory.
"Your band sounds great," said
Swinging Sally. "Please can
we join?"

"Of course!" boomed Henry.
"In fact, I think we're ready
to start."

Henry flapped his ears as loud as he could, and with a stomping, clomping, slithering, sliding, splashing, crashing, furious flapping, the animals made the loudest jungle music that they could.

FLAP

TRUMPETY

Henry was delighted that everyone
wanted to join his band. He was so
happy and excited that he let out an
enormous (and very surprising)
TRUMPETY-TRUMPETY-TRUMP!
Henry was delighted!

The jungle band was ready to play at last.
And what a band! Their music could be
heard throughout the jungle. It got louder
and louder...

But the HUGEST noise in the band was

TRUMPETY-
TRUMPETY-
TRUMP!

It was the best jungle band ever.